Billy's Luck

PAUL SHIPTON

Illustrated by Pat McCarthy

Oxford University Press

OXFORD
UNIVERSITY PRESS

Great Clarendon Street, Oxford OX2 6DP

Oxford University Press is a department of the Unversity of Oxford.
It furthers the University's objective of excellence in research, scholarship,
and education by publishing worldwide in

Oxford New York

Auckland Bangkok Buenos Aires Cape Town Chennai
Dar es Salaam Delhi Hong Kong Istanbul Karachi Kolkata
Kuala Lumpur Madrid Melbourne Mexico City Mumbai Nairobi
São Paulo Shanghai Taipei Tokyo Toronto

Oxford is a registered trade mark of Oxford University Press
in the UK and in certain other countries

ISBN 0 19 916874 1

Printed in Great Britain

Illustrations by Pat McCarthy c/o J Martin & Artists Ltd.

Chapter 1

Our football team is Beaver Road
Juniors. It's the worst team ever. I
should know. I play for them.

We were playing Cogs Lane Juniors
and the match was going better than
usual. The last time we played them
they had beaten us SEVEN-NIL. But by
half-time in this game, they were only
three goals up. Not bad!

As we walked out for the second half,
we were feeling hopeful.

My name's Joel. That's me carrying the ball for the kick-off. Good-looking, aren't I? (Don't answer!)

The kid with glasses is called Alex. He's my best friend, but he's a terrible footballer.

It's funny really – he knows lots of stuff in books ... but he doesn't know how to kick a ball.

The whistle blew and the second half began.

Cogs Lane took a while to warm up – it was a full two minutes before they scored another goal.

Kev, our captain, kicked off again and passed the ball to me. I moved up on the left wing.

The crowd went wild with excitement.
(Well, as wild as they ever get.)

I looked up. Ravi, our striker, was free,
so I passed to him. He trapped the ball
and charged up the left wing with it.
He's the fastest runner I've ever seen.

Then, just as he was about to cross
the ball into the box,

he fell over.

It's always the same story. That's
Ravi's problem – he's fast, but he always
falls over.

Cogs Lane got the ball and scored again.

The rest of the game went on in the same way.

Alex says a good team should be like a well-oiled machine. Our machine must be broken. We normally just charge after the ball in a big group. Alex says that that's how people played football when it was first invented. No rules, no sides – just a huge mob charging after one ball.

So at least we're keeping up tradition – we play football as it used to be played.

Later in the game Ravi passed the ball back to Alex in defence. Big mistake. As usual, Alex was thinking – about computers or maths, or something else that I try NOT to think about.

He never even noticed the ball as it bounced off his leg.

Cogs Lane scored again.

Luke, our goalie, let in goal after goal.

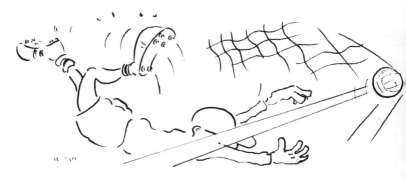

To be fair, I think he had a bad day.

When the final whistle blew, Cogs Lane Juniors had won by nine goals to nil.

If a TV reporter had asked me how I felt, I know what I would have said.

Chapter 2

After the game I walked home with Alex.

It's hard to tell Alex the truth about how bad he is at football. I'd hate to hurt his feelings.

Just then, a voice called out to us.

I always knew Beaver Road Juniors were bad, but I never knew how bad. You were terrible! Pathetic!

It was Steven Snape. He was captain of Longfield Road Juniors.

Everyone knew they were the best team in the area. They won the Championship every year.

We had never beaten them. We had never even SCORED against them.

Joel... as ever you showed the speed and footballing skills of a three-toed sloth.

Steven wasn't trying to be nice. Alex knows all about animals – he told me that a three-toed sloth is an animal which just lazes about up a tree and hardly moves all day long.

It can't be much good at football, can it?

And as for you, Alex ... you're the worst player I've ever seen. The team would be better off without you.

This was too much for me. Before I could stop myself I blurted it out.

'Shut up, Snape! We play you in two weeks. You're going to get a big shock. You wait and see!'

Steven Snape was truly surprised at what I had said. (So was I, to be honest, but I couldn't back down now.)

Yes, I do.

What? You really think Beaver Road can beat us.

Steve giggled nastily.

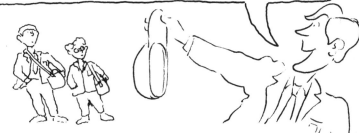

Huh! If your team beats Longfield Road, I'll eat my hat with gravy and mash!

He walked off down the road, smirking.

I just looked at Alex.

Oops! I didn't mean to say that.

Never mind. I heard there's a new kid in Miss Foster's class.

He's going to be at Wednesday's training session. He's supposed to be good.

The following Wednesday we found HOW good the new kid was.

Wednesday practice was usually just a laugh. It was a chance to swap jokes and chat. And if we felt like it, we kicked the ball about.

But today was different. No one messed about. We just watched in amazement as the new kid dazzled us with his footballing skills. He wasn't just good – he was BRILLIANT!

His name was Billy Bryson, and he didn't look like a brilliant footballer – he had skinny legs and knobbly knees. But when he got the ball ...

Tackling, passing, dribbling, heading, shooting ... he could do them all.

When he ran with the ball, it was as if it was glued to his boots.

He could shoot and score with either foot.

It was wonderful to watch. When Billy Bryson played football, he made it look like something more than just a game – it was like art or poetry or something like that. It was beautiful.

Alex and I stood and watched. We were amazed, but we tried to act cool.

What do you think then?

Hm. Not bad. Let's give him a go.

Then we just grinned at each other. We knew that he was best player we had ever seen. Maybe – just maybe – our luck had changed.

After practice, we ran to talk to Billy
Bryson.

Where did you learn to play like that?

Billy shrugged his shoulders.

Dunno. I've always loved playing, so I practise a lot. That's all.

I didn't say that Alex had practised for
years, and he still wasn't any good at
soccer. (I wasn't either, for that matter.)
I was just glad Billy wasn't big-headed
about how good he was.

Alex went on. 'Wow, with you in the team I bet your old school won every game, didn't it?'

My friend's eyes were bright, and I knew what he was thinking. It was as if I could see through his head, right into his brain, and read his thoughts: win, win, we could really win a game!

But Billy Bryson just shook his head.

'I had a lot of bad luck last season,' he said darkly.

Then he got on his bike and cycled off home.

We just stood there. What did he mean?

Chapter 3

We had our next match on Saturday.

Usually we were quite relaxed before a match. There's no point getting worked up, when you know you're going to lose.

But everything was different this week. There was a feeling of excitement in the air. I was so excited I could hardly do up my laces!

Billy Bryson was the only one who wasn't worried. He just took his kit out from his bag. That's when the smell hit my nose.

Hey, what's that smell?

Er, sorry... it must be my lucky socks.

Your lucky socks? What do you mean?

I couldn't believe my ears. Billy nodded.

'I'm a bit superstitious,' he said, going red. 'I have to wear my lucky socks, so I can play my best.'

I shrugged.

'Let's hope they work,' I said and carried on getting changed. It was nearly time for the match.

That afternoon something amazing happened.

No, aliens didn't land in the centre of London.

A great white shark didn't attack swimmers in the local swimming pool.

A vampire didn't come to school to bite the neck of the headteacher (unfortunately).

What happened was much more amazing …

We won the match!

I'll say that again, just to make sure you got it:

WE WON THE MATCH!

Primrose Hill Primary couldn't believe it. The crowd couldn't believe it.

But most of all, after losing so many matches, WE couldn't believe it.

Of course, it was all because of Billy. He was even better than in the practice session.

He ran rings around the other team's midfield.

He zipped past their defenders as if they were statues.

He was incredible.

What's more, the rest of us played better than usual. We didn't all become good footballers in a flash, of course. But everyone seemed to raise their game a bit.

We scored four goals, and Billy got them all. We won 4–2.

If a TV reporter had asked me how I felt, I know what I would have said.

Over the moon, John!

On the way home I told Alex all about Billy and his good-luck socks.

Alex knew about them already. 'And that's not all. He always wears his shirt inside-out before every match … for good luck.'

Alex sounded worried, but I couldn't see the problem.

'I don't care if he wears a ballet outfit and Wellington boots,' I said. 'Just as long as he plays like he did today.'

But Alex went on. '… And he carries a bagful of lucky mascots with him. And he never walks under ladders or steps on the cracks on the pavement.'

I still didn't understand what Alex was getting at.

> Okay, he's a bit superstitious. So what?

Alex spoke to me as though I was a little kid. (I hate it when he does that.)

> So...when somebody is so superstitious, sooner or later their luck runs out. And then what?

Now I was worried. Billy Bryson's luck COULDN'T run out. Not when our next match was against Steven Snape and Longfield Road Juniors.

Chapter 4

Alex is no good at football, but he's smart and he's right about most things.

Unfortunately he was right this time as well.

It was the day of the big match against Longfield Road Juniors. Kick-off was only twenty minutes away, and Billy Bryson – our star player – still hadn't turned up. Worry began to nibble away inside my stomach.

The door burst open. It was Billy Bryson, but he had never looked like this before. His eyes were wide open, and his hands shook. He was in a terrible panic.

'What's wrong?' asked Kev, our captain.

'My lucky socks!' wailed Billy. 'My mum took them to the launderette and lost them! All my luck has gone! Worse than that ... it's BAD luck!'

Alex gave me an I-told-you-so look.
My heart sank.

'I can't play today,' Billy went on.
'Not now ...'

'You've GOT to play,' said Kev. 'The
substitute didn't show up – he's got a
cold. It's just a silly superstition. It
doesn't really mean anything ... You're
still our best player.'

Billy just shook his head.

It took fifteen minutes, but at last he agreed to play. I wasn't any happier. As we walked out to the pitch, it was clear that Billy was a different kid.

I saw Steven Snape and that didn't make me feel any better.

The match started, and the first time Billy got the ball, he tried to pass it to our striker. He mis-kicked and the ball went straight to a Longfield player.

Longfield ran up the pitch and scored. To make things worse, it was Steven Snape who got the goal.

This doesn't look good, I thought.

But there was worse to come. Billy played terribly.

He missed headers,

he tripped over,

he scored an own-goal.

He was useless.
He was playing like one of us!
The football magic was gone.

At half-time we were four goals down.
It felt like old times again – bad old
times.

Billy Bryson hung his head as he
walked off the pitch.

But Alex had run off. He raced up to Billy Bryson, panting hard (Alex wasn't very fit).

'Come with me,' gasped Alex.

The second half began. Would it be another terrible forty-five minutes for us?

Steven Snape kicked off for Longfield Road. He tapped the ball to their Number 6.

He was looking around for someone to pass to, when –

whoosh! – the ball disappeared from his feet.

It was Billy Bryson!

Billy had taken the ball
brilliantly, and was zooming up the
right wing with it.

He beat one player, then another. He
cut inside the box, raced past three
defenders, dribbled around the goalie...

… and blasted the ball into the back of the net. It was a fantastic goal!

As Longfield Road's goalie fetched the ball from the back of the net, I trotted over to Alex.

'What did you say?' I asked. 'How did you get him to stop worrying about his lucky socks?'

Alex tapped the side of his head with one finger (to show how brainy he is).

'I didn't even try,' he said. 'But I gave him an older, smellier, LUCKIER pair of socks to play in. I told him they were the socks Ryan King wore when he won the Cup Final.'

Ryan King was the top striker in the local top team, Grantford United.

How did you get hold of Ryan King's socks?

You mean they're not really lucky?

I didn't. Those are my dad's old gardening socks.

Alex grinned at the look on my face.

Then Alex smiled and winked at me.

The whistle blew and play started again. Billy Bryson got the ball and made a superb run down the middle of the field.

That's all really, except for one thing ...

... did we win that afternoon?

What do you think?

About the author

When I was growing up in Manchester, I always wanted to be an astronaut, a footballer, or (if those didn't work out for any reason) perhaps a rock star. So it came as something of a shock when I became first a teacher and then an editor of educational books.

I have lived in Cambridge, Aylesbury, Oxford and Istanbul. I'm still on the run and now live in Chicago with my wife and family.

One of the characters in this book is based on me. But I'm not saying which one!

Other books at Stages 12, 13, and 14 include:

Cool Clive by Michaela Morgan
Call 999! by Sylvia Moody
Front Page Story by Roger Stevens
Pet Squad by Paul Shipton
Sing for your Supper by Nick Warburton

Also available in packs
Stages 12/13/14 pack A   0 19 916879 2
Stages 12/13/14 class pack A   0 19 916880 6